Mary Anne

Stacey

Dawn

SECRET SANTA

ANN M. MARTIN

SCHOLASTIC INC.
New York Toronto London Auckland Sydney

Library of Congress Cataloging-in-Publication Data

Martin, Ann M., 1955-
  Secret Santa / Ann M. Martin.
    p. cm. -- (The Baby-sitters Club)
    Summary: The members of the Baby-sitters Club draw names to be Secret Santas and grant
each other's holiday wishes, in a series of letters.

[1. Babysitters--Fiction. 2. Christmas--Fiction. 3. Hanukkah--Fiction. 4. Friendship--Fiction. 5. Letters--Fiction.]
I. Title. II. Series: Martin, Ann M., 1955- Baby-sitters Club.
PZ7.M3567585Tp 1994
[Fic]--dc20
                                                                                        93-48981
                                                                                        CIP
                                                                                        AC

Art direction and book design by Elizabeth B. Parisi

Interior Illustrations
David Tommasino p. 3; Michael Sours p. 4; Hollie Rubin pp. 5–6, 11–12, 19; Yan Nascimbene p. 8; Ed Acuna p. 9; FPG International Corp. pp. 14, 25, cover photo; Kevin Bapp p. 15; Nancy Didion p. 17; Madalina Stefan-Stephenson p. 18; Peggy Tegel p. 20; Hodges Soileau p. 23; Ann Wilson p. 26; Philip Scheuer pp. 27–28; Dawn Antoinello pp. 29–30; Carol Newsom p. 31; Ed Parker p. 32
Cover Portraits by Hodges Soileau.

Library of Congress Cataloging-in-Publication Data

ISBN 0-590-48295-5

12 11 10 9 8 7 6 5 4 3 2 1   4 5 6 7 8 9/9

Printed in Singapore

First Scholastic printing, October 1994

KAREN

DEAR SANTA,

HI. MY NAME IS KAREN BREWER. I AM SEVEN YEARS OLD. THIS IS WHAT I WANT FOR CHRISTMAS.

1. DIAPER BABY AND DIAPER BABY BATH AND CHANGING CENTER
2. CHARLIE AND THE CHOCOLATE FACTORY BY MR. ROALD DAHL (I HAD ANOTHER COPY BUT MY BROTHER DROPPED IT IN HIS SPIGATTI AT SUPPER)
3. MY TOUCH 'N' TYPE TYPEWRITER BY MATCO® LIKE ON TELEVISION
4. THE LITTLE GENERAL STORE BY MATCO® LIKE ON TELEVISION
5. DEAR MR. HENSHAW BY MS. BEVERLY CLEARY
6. A SLIEGH BELL LIKE THE BOY GOT FROM MR. C. IN THE POLAR EXPRESS BY MR. CHRIS VAN ALLSBURG
7. PEACE AND NO FIGHTING AND NO GUNS
8. BUILD-A-REAL VOLCANO KIT
9. E-Z-2-DO ART BOX (THE ONE WITH GLITTER PENS AND EXTRA STICKERS AND THE DINOSAUR PENCILS)
10. RAZZ-A-MATAZZ RHINESTONE KIT

I THINK THAT IS ALL, SANTA. I HOPE YOU HAVE A VERY MERRY CHRISTMAS. PLEASE GIVE MY BEST TO MRS. CLAUS AND ALL THE REINDEER, ESPECIALLY ~~RUDOLF~~ RUDOLPH.

YOURS TRULY,
KAREN BREWER

P.S. I HAVE BEEN GIGUNDOLY GOOD THIS YEAR, BUT MY BROTHER HAS NOT.

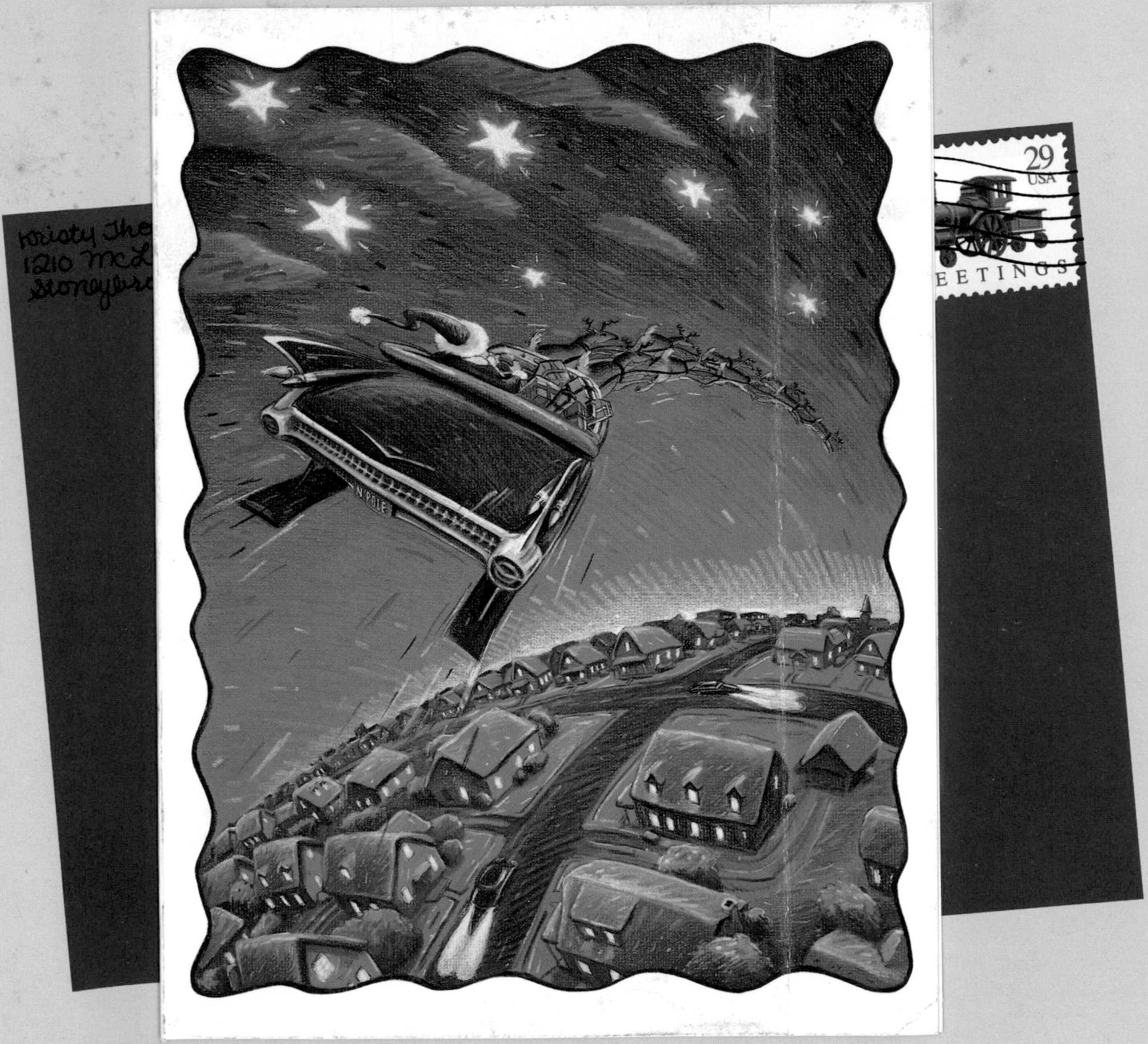
29
USA
N POLE

Miss Eliza Stanley
40 Tenth Street
Apt A
Freeport, CT 06900

Santa Claus
The North Pole

I wish I didn't have such a big mouth. (Seriously.)

Kristy

I wish to be remembered forever.

Mallory ☺

I no this is a hard wish to grant but I wish I could do something meaningful for somebody.

Claudia

I wish I had a better sense of humor.

Shannon

I wish I could be in New York City at Christmastime.

Stacey

I wish Cam Geary would write to me for real. (Not one of these fake letters his secretary sends to all his fans.)

Mary Anne

I wish I could dance with the New York City Ballet.

Jessi

I WISH I COULD HAVE THREE MORE WISHES.

HA, HA.

LOGAN

Dear Dad,

Hi! Merry Christmas! I would feel kind of funny sending a card to you, so I decided to write you a Christmas letter instead. I've never done that before, because we were always together at the holidays. I know I will come to NYC on the day after Christmas, but it doesn't seem the same. I want to be in New York for the Christmas season. Christmas in Stoneybrook will be fine, I guess. It's just that I wanted to see the huge tree go up at Rockefeller Plaza, and I wanted to see the lighting ceremony. Also, I wanted to see the big snowflake when it was first lit. And I wanted to see the windows at Lord and Taylor's. I even wanted to see Santa Claus at Macy's! I know I can see everything with you after Christmas, but that just isn't the same. Plus, I wish I could be with you on Christmas Day. And with Mom, too. That isn't possible since I'm a divorced kid, but wishing never hurt anyone, did it?

Guess what. My friends and I are playing Santa Claus to a disadvantaged girl. Yesterday we bought her a Barbie doll and a book. Since that was all she asked for, and it didn't seem like much, we also bought her an art kit, some silly Santa kneesocks, and an enormous candy cane.

Merry Christmas, and I'll see you soon!

I miss you.

Lots of Love,
Stacey

P.S. My BSC friends and I started a secret Santa project. I drew Logan Bruno's name. Do you have any idea where I can get a four leaf clover at this time of year? (I'll explain later.)

P.P.S. Shannon sent me the silliest riddle. Here it is: How do you know if an elephant has been in your refrigerator?   By the footprints in the cheesecake.

NOËL

Dear Mary Anne,
  Greetings from California! (Don't let this card fool you. It may be sunny here, but it isn't all that warm.) My friends in the We ♡ Kids Club and I are throwing a Christmas party for some of the kids we sit for. Isn't that cool? We already threw a Hanukkah party.
  Well, I know you guys need my secret Santa wish, so here it is:
  I wish my BSC friends and my W♡KC friends could be better friends. You're going to keep this a secret, right, Mary Anne?
  I guess that's all. Oh, wait! Don't forget to send someone's Secret Santa wish for me to grant.
    Love and Sunshine, Your sister Dawn

Ms. Mary Anne Spier
177 Burnt Hill Road
Stoneybrook, CT 06800

Dear Mr. and Mrs. Stanley,

Hi! My name is Kristy Thomas. This year my friends and I decided to get in touch with Happy Child, Inc., and answer a kid's letter to Santa. We got Eliza's letter, and we had a lot of fun shopping for her. We are sending the presents she asked for (the book and the Barbie) plus a few other things, in a separate package. We feel a little bad, though, because we can't grant Eliza's real wish. Eliza said what she __really__ wants is for Jennifer to come home. I'm telling you this because Eliza sent her half of her friendship necklace in the letter. (She thought that would help Santa Claus identify Jennifer.) Anyway, I'm sending it back with the presents, because I'm sure Eliza will want it.

My friends and I hope you have a very merry Christmas!

Sincerely,

Kristy Thomas

Mary Anne Spier

Claudia Kishi

Jessi Ramsey

LOGAN BRUNO

Mallory Pike

Shannon Kilbourne

Stacey McGill

(and Dawn Schafer)

THANK YOU

Hi Dawn!!

Merry Chrismas and Happy hollidays and gretings of the season. How are you more important when are you coming back here? Guess what? You know Eliza Stanly and remerber the letter Kristy got from Mrs. Stanly? Well I have been doing some reserch. I thought we could help Eliza and her sister get together at Chrismas so I looked at wedding anouncments in old newspapers. My mom helped me and I found out Mrs. Stanly's madem name was Ray. So Jennifer must be with a faimly named Ray in New hope. I will keep looking.

Wish me luck!
Claudia

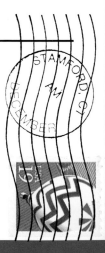

Ms. Dawn Schafer
22 Buena Vista
Palo City California
92800

Dear Shannon

Hi! Gretings form Stoneybrook. How is sking. How are you? You will never guess what is hapening with Eliza Stanly. Remerber she is the girl who wants her sister for Cristmas. Well her mom said Jennifer, thats the sister, has been living with her ant and uncle in Newhope. So I found out the ant and uncle's last name is Ray. Then at our last BSC meeting I looked up the Rays in the New hope phone book there are three. I have been calling them trying to find the right family. But I have been doing it slowly because I fell a little funny about it. Anyway I have called two of them and they were the wrong ones so Jenifer must be with the thrid famly. I will call them as soon as I get the nerve. Wish me luck!

By the way what is with the corny jokes you have been sending everyone? You need a better jokebook. Just kidding ha ha.

Merry Cristmas!
Lots of love,
Claud

P.S. Do you have any idear why Kristy has been asking everyone for old school pictures and stuff like that.

Dear Mr. Geary,
 Or should I call you Cam?
 Hello, It's me, again. Dawn Schafer. Do you remember me? (I'm sure you get a _lot_ of mail.) I wrote you a very important letter last week. The letter was about my step-sister and best friend, Mary Ann Spier, and I told you that I am her Secret Santa this year. Her wish—and she could have wished for anything— was to get a _real_ letter or card from you. So anyway, I hope you received the blank Christmas card I sent with my letter. All you have to do is sign it, and then seal it in the stamped envelope that I also sent. It is addressed to Mary Anne, and when that turns up in her mailbox she will just... well, I'm not sure what she'll do, exactly, but it will be spectacular.

 Thank you again for taking care of this. Your card will make this the best Christmas ever for your biggest fan.
                      Sincerely yours,
                      Dawn Schafer

P E A C E

MISS MALLORY PIKE

134 SLATE STREET

STONEYBROOK, CT 06800

Petersons' Nurseries
17 Old Stoney Point Hollow
Stoneybrook, CT 06800

The New York City Ballet proudly presents

The Nutcracker Suite

Starring...

Jessica Ramsey

Prima Ballerina, our Shining Star!

Merry Christmas, Jessi!
I had this printed up just for you.
Maybe you can't dance with the
New York City Ballet now, but
I bet you will one day.

(Sometimes Christmas wishes
take awhile to come true.)

Love from your Secret Santa,
Shannon

Ms. Jessi Ramsey
612 Fawcett Avenue
Stoneybrook, CT 06800

Dear Santa,
    I have been so good this year, you wood not beleive it. I all ready sent you my Xmas list. But now I have a quesion. well really two quesions. #1 on Xmas eve, when you are flying around all nigth do you get to stop at Mcdonalds for coffee and a hambarger that is what my mom and dad wood order. #2 where do your raindeer go to the bathroom? I realy need to know.
                    Love, Claire Pike

P.S. Remember I have been good all year.

P.P.S. My sister Margo is writing this for me.

Kristy Thomas
1210 McLelland Road
Stoneybrook, CT 06800

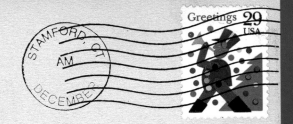

Ms. Dawn Schafer
22 Buena Vista
Palo City, CA 92800

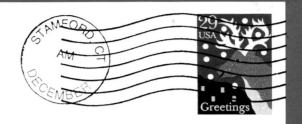

Jennifer Stanley
c/o The Rays
29 Spring Road
New Hope, CT 06800

Eliza Stanley
40 Tenth Street
Apt. A
Freeport, CT 06900

Dear Claudia,

Hello, it's me — your Secret Santa.
This note might not seem like much of a
Christmas present, but that's because you made
granting your wish so easy. In fact, you granted it yourself!
Claud, you wished you could do something meaningful
for someone, and you've already done it. You found
Eliza's sister for her and brought them together —
which made this the best Christmas Eliza can remember.
You did it all yourself, too. Kristy and the rest of us
chipped in and bought Eliza her presents. And we _wished_
we could find Jennifer for her. But you were the one
who did it, every step of the way. And look what
happened — magic!

Claud, you do other meaningful things, too. Your
art is meaningful (it inspires people), you give your
friends meaningful gifts, and you made a big
difference in your grandmother's life. You _are_ meaningful.

So, merry Christmas, and thanks for making
your wish so easy to grant!

Your inspired friend,
Mallory

HAPPY·HOLIDAYS

Mallory
i
Claudia

Jessi

Kristy